This Book Belongs To

Andrew-Hume

Also by Michael Mullen

The Viking Princess

The Little Drummer Boy

The Caravan

The Flight of the Earls

The Long March

The Four Masters

Children's
POOLBEG

Marcus the School Mouse

A Note on the Author

Michael Mullen lives in Castlebar, County Mayo. He is a leading historical novelist and the author of many books for young people, on both historical and contemporary themes.

MARCUS
the School Mouse

Michael Mullen

With illustrations by Ann Kennedy

Children's
POOLBEG

First published 1993 by
Poolbeg Press Ltd,
A Division of Poolbeg Enterprises Ltd,
Knocksedan House,
Swords, Co Dublin, Ireland

© Text Michael Mullen 1993
© Illustrations Ann Kennedy 1993

This book was first published to mark the 125th anniversary of the foundation
of the Irish National Teachers' Organisation (INTO)

The moral right of the author has been asserted.

ISBN 1 85371 270 1

A catalogue record for this book is available from the British Library.

Cover design by Poolbeg Press
Set by Mac Book in ITC Stone Serif 12/17
Printed by The Guernsey Press Ltd
Vale, Guernsey, Channel Islands

To all members of the INTO,
past and present

Contents

Contents

1

Old Schools for New

It was an autumn evening. The sun was still hot. It stood in the west like a huge orange. The sky around the sun was the colour of marmalade. The clouds hung above the countryside like meringues. The air was soft and full of scents: of nuts and apples and pears and flowers and the scents that come from small woods. Nature was at its best.

The new school, on the side of a hill, caught the reflection of the sun and the windows were changed to large plates of gold. The walls glowed with fresh paint. The tarmac in the yard glistened.

At the bottom of the hill stood the old school. Great slabs of plaster had fallen from the walls, showing old stones of awkward shapes. The doors were hanging from their hinges and here

and there a window pane had been smashed. Inside, the timber floors, hilled and hollowed and holed and worn thin by shoes and boots, creaked like old bones. When the wind blew, it whistled down the chimney with a frightening cry. The old school had been empty for a whole year. The desks, with the pupils' names carved into the wood, belonged to another time. The pictures and charts on the wall were faded and curled with damp.

The new Principal had visited the school a year before. She knocked on the walls and peered into the cupboards. She tested the floor and turned the taps.

"Leave the place to rot," she advised the board of management. "It's had its day. We will use the community hall until the new school is finished."

"What a cheek," the spider said from the middle of his web, remembering her comments. "This school suits me and it will suit those who come after me."

"True, true," the cockroach replied. He agreed with everything any animal or insect said and besides, he loved dark corners and damp places.

"I don't know. I'll have to think about it," Marcus the school mouse said.

"There is nothing to think about," the spider insisted. "We have the place to ourselves. I can survive here for the rest of my life. Now with all the children gone, I can build cobwebs wherever I like. Cobwebs on the ceiling, cobwebs on the walls, cobwebs on the legs of desks and cobwebs in all the presses. There never was a better time for cobwebs."

"Good riddance to the children, I say," said the cockroach. "I never liked children and they never liked me. I took my life in my claws every time I crossed the floor. I was definitely an endangered species."

But Marcus, the mouse with the white ears that had often glowed in the past, had other ideas. He was a mouse who thought a lot. While the others waited for him to speak, they continued talking among themselves.

"Knowledge is useless," the spider said. "All I need to know is how to build a web and trap a fly."

"I have a small head and a small brain," the cockroach added. "With me it's in one ear and out the other. But Marcus there has a large head that holds a lot of information. And he has the advantage that his ears glow in the dark."

"*Used* to glow," corrected Marcus.

Marcus could remember well when his ears glowed like great bulbs. They would light up the whole school at night. But since the children disappeared, there were no sweets or treats to be had and his ears had lost their glow.

He had grown tired of his two companions during the summer holidays. The cockroach talked of nothing but cobwebs and the spider was always complaining about his health and safety. So on this autumn evening, he made up his mind. "I'm going to leave this place. There's no future for me here."

"What?" said the spider and the cockroach together.

"There's no future for me here," repeated Marcus.

"Well, there *is* for me," the spider said.

"And I'm happy where I am," added the cockroach.

"I think I'll go and take up residence in the new school," Marcus continued thoughtfully.

The spider and the cockroach could not believe their ears. "You are foolish, Marcus," said the spider.

The cockroach continued, "Old schools are

best suited to mice. Just look around you. This room is full of crevices where you can make your home. You can live under the floorboards or behind the skirting or in the old cupboards. You are spoiled for choice."

"Tomorrow I move," said Marcus firmly. "Since the children left this school, I haven't had a decent meal. I remember evenings when I sat down to a dinner of crisps followed by chocolate, and all washed down by a lake of orange left by some infant. Those were the days. Now I am hungry and I've lost weight. My ears no longer glow. They need energy and I can get that energy only from chocolate. Oh, for a square of chocolate: the thought makes my mouth water. There is no food here any longer. At night I have to venture out just in order to keep body and soul together. And I fear Tigris the cat, who is always on the prowl. So my mind is made up."

"You'll be back. Mark my words," the spider warned him.

They argued for an hour but Marcus would not listen to the other two. "Tomorrow I'm off. I'll do better on high ground. There'll be more sunshine in the new building. And I'm in dire need of a good meal. There are nights when I dream of crisps and chocolate."

Once Marcus had made up his mind, he was happy. He would give up the old and go in search of the new.

2

The Power Returns

The following evening, Marcus slipped out of the old school through a broad hole in the door. He looked cautiously about. Tigris the cat was nowhere to be seen. He ran across the old yard. Nettles and docks and briars had taken root in the tarmac and already the surface was running with cracks. He looked back at the old school that he was deserting. It seemed so old that he was sure it must have been there since the beginning of the world.

For a moment, he felt a sense of regret. "You would be safer in the old school, you know," said a voice in his head.

"Go on, go west and up the hill," another voice answered.

He followed the advice of the second voice,

but moving very cautiously. Tigris was always about somewhere, ready to spring. Sure enough, he heard a rush through the undergrowth on the edge of the yard. With a spring, he reached the pipe that drained the water from the tarmac to the gully at the side of the road. A great nailed paw tried to scrape at him but he was out of reach. Then Tigris put his nose to the end of the pipe. His breath was foul, smelling of meat.

If Marcus had had the energy he would have flashed his ears and blinded the cat, but they had not glowed for a long time. He badly needed chocolate.

He hoped it would not rain before the cat grew tired of stalking him. A sudden downpour and he would be swept through the pipe and into the gully and down into some dark cave where the sun never shone. It took him time to catch his breath and much longer to gather his courage. Finally he emerged from the pipe and crossed out of the yard on to the side of the road.

The road seemed vast to Marcus. He remembered the safe cross code, which he had heard the children repeating many times in the classroom. He looked right and left and right again. With a little rush he was in the middle

of the road and standing in a puddle of diesel oil. The fumes rushed to his head and made him dizzy and confused. When he looked at the oil, his eyes were filled with flashing colours.

Then it happened. Down the road raced a monster. He froze. The monster was upon him and past him. He gulped and rushed on to the far side of the road.

"That was a close shave," a bumble bee remarked to Marcus.

"You can say that again!"

"That was a close shave," repeated the bee.

"Don't say that again. I still have the shivers from thinking about it."

"You were one of the lucky ones. I've seen mice flattened on that road. Their eyes were flattened and their tails were flattened. They looked like photographs instead of animals. Of course, I'm lucky, I can fly over the road."

The picture of the flattened mice shook Marcus to the core. For an instant his ears glowed.

"I may be wrong, but did your ears just glow?" the curious bee asked.

"Perhaps. In the old days," Marcus continued sadly, "they glowed every night like a lighthouse. But I need lots of energy to make them glow and for the past while I have been lacking energy. I've lost weight and my nerves are in shreds."

"Try to make them glow again," the bumble bee begged. "I'd love to see it."

"I can't. I need energy."

"Would honey give you energy?"

Marcus brightened. "Oh, yes."

"I can show you where a man hid a honeycomb he had just taken from a hive. He is supposed to be back for it this evening on his way home, but he won't know if you take a little bit."

They found the honeycomb as the bumble bee said, hidden in a corner of the ditch. Marcus ate all he could and then, the honey dripping from his whiskers, he concentrated hard and pushed the energy into his ears. The bumble bee was knocked over by the powerful glow.

"Are you sure you're not a mouse from outer space?" he asked when he had recovered.

"No," said Marcus. "I'm a simple school mouse who has decided to leave the old school and move to the new one."

Then there was a tearing noise. Tigris the cat appeared on the road from nowhere and rushed at Marcus. Marcus made his ears glow. The cat stopped in his tracks and backed away. Marcus

chased him away, all the time making his ears glow like headlights. He returned to the bumble bee, worn out.

"I still have the power," he said, "but now I have used up all my energy. I feel faint. I'll have some more honey to take me as far as my new home."

When he had finished eating he said goodbye to the bumble bee and set off up the hill towards where the new school was situated. He found a warm dry place under a tree, curled up and fell asleep.

3

Aoife the Pine Marten

It was midday when Marcus awoke. The sun was hot and he felt well-rested. He sat up and listened. He could hear sounds rolling down the hill from the new school. Breathing deeply, he filled his lungs with air.

"The air is delicious, simply delicious," he said to himself.

"It's always delicious up here," a voice answered from close by. It was a pine marten.

"I am Marcus, the school mouse," Marcus introduced himself.

"Glad to meet you. I'm Aoife the pine marten. I live close to the forest. I am one of the very few pine martens left in this country. I saw your ears glow last evening. I was very impressed. Are you a space mouse?"

"No, I'm a simple school mouse. I'm leaving the old school to go and live in the new school."

"I see. Will you make your ears glow? I'm dying to see them again."

"I'm afraid I can't. I haven't enough energy. Were it not for a bumble bee who found me some honey to eat, I could not have glowed last evening. He saved my life. Tigris the cat attacked me but I sent him packing."

"I don't like cats either," said Aoife. "Where does this one live?"

"He still hangs around the old school. I believe he tried to get the official cat position in the new building but the Principal gave him a boot on his tail and sent him packing."

"So you're the school mouse?" said Aoife. "I've heard of school mice but I've never met one before."

"Well, I was the official school mouse in the old school," said Marcus.

Marcus and Aoife talked for some time at the edge of a narrow path through the forest, not too far from the school.

"Do you think you'll find a nice home in this school?" his new friend asked Marcus. "I watched them build it. Solid block it is. Every hole has been sealed. I can't see you getting in."

"There's always a way in. I've never known a mouse that could not break into a school. It's part of our training."

"Then I'll go along with you to see how you get on. It's best to wait until evening. You wouldn't try to break in while the children are in school?"

"No, it's far too dangerous."

They talked some more. It was a pleasant day and there was not much else to do. Finally the sound of children rolled down the hill.

"They're on their way home," said Marcus.

They waited half an hour more. Some children had stayed on to kick football in the yard. Marcus and Aoife heard the noise of the ball on the new tarmac. Finally it stopped.

Marcus and Aoife set off, with Marcus in the lead and Aoife keeping a look-out in case Tigris made a sudden attack from behind. They ran up the new school wall and down the far side and found themselves in the middle of a sea of tarmac.

The school looked clean and new. Not a crisp bag or a chocolate wrapper was to be seen. "The place is too clean," Aoife observed.

"Give it another month," Marcus answered wisely. "There will be plenty of litter then and where there is litter there is delicious food, crisps and chocolate. I bet you if I can find a way inside there'll be a rubbish bin and in that rubbish bin will be the finest meal a mouse ever set eyes on."

The two new friends surveyed the school as two bank robbers might survey a bank.

"Beats me how you're going to get in," said Aoife finally.

"Where there's a will, there's a way!"

"When I see it, I'll believe it."

"Let me study the building close up," said Marcus.

He and Aoife moved across the fresh black tarmac, closer to the school. They examined the doors but there was not a hole in sight. They were well sealed against wind and rain. Then they studied the windows but they too were well sealed.

"You've had it, Marcus," said Aoife. "They knew you were coming."

"I'm telling you there's a weakness somewhere. There always is."

Then he saw it. "The bad workman is the mouse's best friend. Don't look down: look up.

I can get in under the eaves. I see a hole."

Aoife narrowed her eyes but she could see nothing.

"Watch this," Marcus said.

Like a flash he scampered up the pebble-dashed wall and disappeared. Five minutes later he appeared at the window. He tried to say something to Aoife but the windows were double-glazed so he had to make his way back along the attic and down the wall.

"It was a piece of cake," he said modestly. "And I have discovered the waste bin. I could smell the food. It is like a hotel larder. Tonight I will eat my fill."

"Be careful," Aoife advised. "I doubt if a mouse is a welcome guest at a new school. They have all sorts of traps and poison these days."

"I'll be careful."

It was time to say goodbye. Before she left, Aoife reminded Marcus, "Tonight, if your energy comes back, will you make your ears glow from the window?"

"Certainly, certainly."

With that, Aoife was gone.

Aoife waited for two hours in the evening behind the wall outside the school. As it was

getting dark, two great glowing ears pulsed like searchlights in a window. Aoife knew then that Marcus had discovered a store of chocolate. She made her way home, contented.

4

A New Home

It was morning when Marcus awoke from a most happy dream. It was a chocolate-coloured dream set in a country where chocolate grew in the fields like daisies and fell from the skies like rain.

His energy had been partly restored. But with the evening flashing of his ears to Aoife, it had fallen again the way a battery goes flat. He scuttled along the rafters, found a small hole in the ceiling and scampered down a wall and into a rubbish bin. He munched happily on a square of chocolate, feeling energy pouring into his body. Life felt good and promised to be even better.

The school was silent.

Then it was silent no longer.

A door opened.

Marcus heard someone singing.

He darted up the side of the litter bin and peered over the edge. He saw a teacher at her desk. From the way she behaved, Marcus guessed that she was the new Principal. She was tall and thin, with a blue suit, a white shirt and a bow at her neck.

"I smell trouble," Marcus said to himself. "I don't think she will like a mouse in her school."

Marcus had time to look around and realised that he was in an office, not a classroom. There were lots of machines. There was a photocopying machine by the wall which the Principal now used to copy a hand-out. On top of the sheet was the heading *Rules and Regulations*. Marcus could not read the rest from the waste bin, but the rules looked very serious and severe.

In a corner of the office was a television set and underneath it a video recorder. There were other machines, all spanking new and shining white, but they made no sense to Marcus, because he had never seen their like in the old school. But he had the feeling that they were all going to make life a bit more difficult for himself and for the children.

While the Principal gazed down at the sheets

rolling off the photocopier, Marcus scuttled up the wall and back into the attic. He made his way to the hole by which he had entered the evening before and looked at the children coming into the yard. They were all wearing the new school uniform, a grey jumper with a crest and grey trousers or skirts.

At exactly half past nine, an alarm sounded, an alarm that would frighten a cat. For a moment Marcus thought the school was on fire and he sniffed to see whether he could smell smoke. Then he realised that it was the signal for school to begin. He quickly found another route down from the attic that didn't lead to the Principal's office and found himself peering out from a cupboard into a classroom.

There was clattering and chattering in that room especially because it was the infants' classroom. Chairs fell over and desks scraped the floor, and the small children didn't know where to sit. When they were put in their seats some of them wandered about and others began to cry. The infant teacher took out a jar of lollipops and soon peace was restored.

Marcus watched the children suck the lollipops. They wrapped their tongues around them, making them wet and sticky.

Then one little girl let her lollipop fall behind the radiator. It was safely stuck half way down. The girl began to howl. "Lots more where that came from," the teacher said cheerfully, handing her a new red lollipop.

Marcus could smell the lollipop from his hiding place. He was delighted. "I'll have it tonight for dessert," he promised himself.

He was on the look-out for his main course. As soon as the children got busy with their drawing and the teacher's attention was on them, he sneaked around and peeped into their bags. The parents had packed the school lunches in plastic containers so he could only guess at what was in them. Once or twice he was sure he caught sight of the outline of a chocolate bar. But he would have to wait until lunch-break to see what was on the menu.

Break-time finally came. The teacher told the children to take out their lunches. "Don't touch your food until I tell you," he said. He wanted everyone to start eating at the same time. But one child had already flattened out the tinfoil wrapper to display ham sandwiches. They made Marcus's mouth water. Definitely there were the makings of a good meal in this classroom.

Marcus was particularly interested in the careless eaters. They broke off parts of the sandwiches and let them fall on the ground. During lunchtime, bread and meat and crumbs of biscuits began to fall under the chairs. There was food enough for Marcus for a week.

At the end of the break, all the crumbs and bits and pieces were swept up by two of the children with the help of the teacher. Everything was put into the bin. "Perfect, absolutely perfect," thought Marcus. But at that moment he was carried away by his pleasure and let himself be seen by one of the children.

"Mouse, mouse," the little boy called to the teacher. They all looked in his direction. Marcus was in a corner but he couldn't run and hide without crossing the floor. He was aware of thirty pairs of eyes looking at him. "Mouse, mouse," all the children called, waving and pointing. He had blown his cover on his first day in the new school.

"Where?" asked the teacher, in a nervous voice.

"In the corner, teacher," said one child.

"He has yellow ears, teacher," said her

neighbour.

"He has pink ears," insisted a little boy in the back row.

"Silence, children. Are you sure you saw a mouse? Cross your hearts and promise that you are telling the truth."

They crossed their hearts and told the truth. Marcus knew what would come next. While all the children were looking up at the teacher, he managed to cross the floor and hide in the cupboard again.

The children were sent into the yard. The infant teacher left the classroom and returned with the tall, thin Principal.

"I just can't teach in a classroom with a mouse. It makes me too nervous. I have a thing about mice."

"Don't worry, Mr White, leave it to me. I will take steps. I know there is a cat still hanging around the old school. Tigris is his name. I was hoping we could do without a cat here—all the buildings were supposed to be completely sealed and mouse-proof. It just proves that mice can get in anywhere. Now we'll have to get the cat up here."

Marcus trembled. Things were looking bad.

He had to make plans.

"I'll get the cat this evening. I'll put him in the attic. The mouse must have got in through there. I'll not have mice in this nice new school."

At three o'clock the school alarm rang again. Marcus was still cooped up in the cupboard, afraid to move a whisker. The children poured out of the classrooms and made their way down to the gate to the awaiting cars and the school bus.

There was a terrible silence, and Marcus knew that it was the calm before the storm or before a great battle.

He needed energy. As soon as the teacher left the infant classroom, he scuttled over to the bin. He ate as many sweets, biscuit-crumbs and pieces of chocolate as he could. He was bulging with food and buzzing with energy as he made his way back up to the attic.

Later that evening, in the dark, the Principal came back to the school with Tigris. She talked to Tigris as if he were human. "Now, Tigris, I have work for you. Somewhere in the school— I think probably up in the attic—there is a nasty mouse. I want you to destroy him. You can start looking in the attic."

Tigris mewed with pleasure.

The Principal got a ladder, lifted the trap-door and pushed Tigris into the attic. She left the door open.

Then she left the school. Marcus could hear her car driving away.

Marcus was ready. He drew on half his energy. It rushed to his ears. He made them glow like beacons.

Tigris panicked when he saw the blinding light. He rushed around the attic, completely confused. He jumped through the trap-door and fled into a broom cupboard in the hall. The next morning, the Principal found him, still shivering, in a corner.

She studied the cat.

All the teachers studied the cat.

The Principal shook her head. "He looks to me as if he has had a nervous breakdown," she said. Tigris was taken away to a vet who understood these things.

Later, Marcus heard the Principal talking to the staff. "There is more here than meets the eye. I'll have to report to the board of management."

Marcus had won the first round.

5

The Board of Management

It was late one evening that the meeting was held, in the staffroom of the new school.

"We have a problem, a serious problem," the Principal told the board of management.

"Disruptive pupils?" one of the board members asked.

"No, more serious than that, I'm afraid," the Principal replied.

"Blocked toilets?" another lady suggested.

"No. More serious than that," the Principal said again.

"A plague in the school?"

"Almost as serious as that."

"Somebody stole our funds?"

"No. But about as serious as that."

The meeting was getting very excited.

"Tell us," the members demanded with one voice.

"We have a mouse in the school."

They gasped.

"A mouse in the school!" they said together.

"Yes, a mouse in the school. He has been seen. He has pink, or white, or grey, or yellow ears."

"This is terrible!" one of the board of management members said. "How did he get into the school? I thought it was supposed to be mouse-proof."

"So did I," the Principal replied.

"And so did we all," the members of the board chorused.

There was silence for a moment.

Then the priest spoke. "We must get rid of the mouse."

"I second that," said the dentist.

"I third it," said the postmistress.

"I fourth it," said the mechanic.

"I fifth it," said the sweetshop lady.

"And I have the pleasure of sixthing it," said the garda, who always liked to have the last word.

Again there was silence.

"I suggest that we put Tigris the cat from the

old school in the new building," said the postmistress, who often fed Tigris. "He is a fierce mouse-hunter. No mouse has ever escaped him."

"We have already tried Tigris," the Principal said sadly.

"And what happened?" asked the priest. "Did Tigris fail?"

"Not only did he fail but he has had a nervous breakdown. He's now in the care of the vet, Mrs Brophy," the Principal answered.

All the members of the board of management considered what the Principal had told them. They chewed it about in their heads as children chew gum.

"Are you certain Tigris failed?" asked the post mistress.

"He's just a bundle of nerves. He's in a cat hospital, Mrs Brophy tells me."

"We must come up with a plan," the garda said severely. "If one mouse has found his way into the school, then others will follow."

"News will spread," agreed the dentist, "and nothing spreads faster than mouse news. Every mouse within ten miles will make a bee-line for the school. We will be overrun like they were by the rats in Hamelin."

"Then let's get a piper to play them out of the place," suggested the priest. "I know a good piper. He plays at matches and leads parades."

"It would cost too much," the Principal replied. "Besides, you remember what happened at Hamelin."

They were silent again. They sat like wax figures around the table. Then they all began to talk together. From the attic, Marcus listened to their talk. What he heard made his blood run cold. Each of them had a suggestion about how to get rid of Marcus.

"I say we should build small guillotines," said the garda. "I could rig them up in no time. Put some cheese on a little platform and—crash! Off with his head."

"I believe that he should die by drowning," suggested the sweetshop lady. She explained in detail her idea that the mouse should be tipped head-first into a bucket of water. She said she had used this plan successfully when she was bothered by mice in her shop and that no mouse had ever dared to come back inside her door.

"No, poisoning is the only cure," declared the dentist. "I have a poison at home that would kill an elephant."

"There is a new trap on the market," said the garda. "It has teeth like a shark's. It would cut the mouse in two. I saw it on television."

"We should use the most modern techniques, I believe," said the mechanic, who had been silent until now. "Let's blast him out with a new gizmo I got from America. It shatters a mouse's brains instantly. I have one in my attic."

They all listened to the mechanic, who rarely spoke, and declared that his idea was the best one of the night. They voted unanimously to follow it.

The meeting was brought to an end by the Principal, but not before five hundred pounds, raised in a raffle by members of the board of management, was placed in the school safe. Only the Principal was to know the combination and all the others turned their backs while she opened and closed the heavy safe.

"We have now raised three thousand pounds for the school," she said proudly. "We can improve our beautiful school even more with three thousand pounds."

Marcus watched the members of the board of management leave. Soon the school was dark and silent again.

"What a bloodthirsty lot they are. I am just a simple school mouse, wanting to live in peace with everyone."

The Principal believed that she had now found the perfect way to get rid of Marcus. The next morning she brought a strange black box into the staffroom. She explained to the teachers how it worked and that she had borrowed it from the mechanic. They were impressed by its size.

"The gizmo inside will blow the mouse's brains apart," she stated.

Marcus listened to the horrible talk. By now he was very familiar with the new school and he could find a pipe, a cupboard or a drawer in which to hide in almost every room. He knew that it was a case of life or death. If he had ever needed energy, he would need it for that evening. He had to have chocolate, and plenty of it. So at lunch-break, he rushed down to the infants' room and ate three half-bars of chocolate that he found abandoned. He ate and ate as he had never eaten before and managed to climb back into the attic only with great difficulty.

He listened as the children came back into the classroom. "Someone stole my chocolate," one

little boy cried.

"And mine," said another boy.

"And mine too," wailed a little girl.

It took the infant teacher half an hour to restore calm and silence to the classroom.

Then another little girl piped up. "It must be the mouse, Sir. Nobody was in the classroom during lunch-hour."

"It must be the mouse, Sir," they all said.

Mr White went out and returned with the Principal. "It's just a small mouse and we will soon be rid of him," the Principal assured the teacher and the children.

That evening when the school was empty, the Principal placed the black box with long wires in the attic. "At seven o'clock," she said to herself, "it will go off, and that will be the end of Mister Mouse."

Then she left the school.

Marcus listened to the time ticking away, very quickly. He looked at the black box.

And then at seven o'clock, he heard a high-pitched sound from the box.

Marcus was ready.

He stood in front of the black box and sent energy into his ears. They glowed for just two seconds like they had never glowed before. It was a huge burst of energy.

The black box exploded without doing any harm to Marcus.

Marcus had defeated the black box and the evil plans of the board of management.

6

Victory

It was the following morning. The Principal and the mechanic, who had so cruelly planned the end of Marcus, arrived at the school very early. It was obvious that they were quite excited. The mouse had caused them trouble for two days, and at night they dreamed of one mouse and one mouse only: the school mouse.

They both rubbed their hands with delight as they left the Principal's car and walked to the door of the school. The Principal eagerly unlocked the door and they rushed down the corridor.

"We'll find him in the attic running around in circles and quite mad. He'll have no memory of the past and no future to speak of," the owner of the gizmo said.

"I couldn't tolerate a mouse in the school. The

children just love mice and will use any excuse to rush around the place after him. And Mr White especially hates mice."

"Don't worry. I can guarantee that no brainless mouse has a chance against this gizmo," the mechanic assured her.

The Principal climbed the ladder and drew the wire attached to the black box towards her. As soon as she gave the first tug, she knew that something was wrong. Then she saw. At the end of the wire dangled the remains of the gizmo. The timbers of the box were in shreds and the gizmo itself lay in tiny useless pieces. There was an evil smell of burning. The Principal stared in disbelief.

"It's impossible, it's impossible," she repeated.

"What's impossible?" asked the gizmo owner, who was standing behind the Principal on the ladder and couldn't see what was going on.

"This," she said, handing down the remains of the black box.

The gizmo owner looked at the remains of the gizmo. "There is only one explanation for this," he said. "A great surge of energy passed through the attic and wrecked the system."

"I don't believe it," whispered the Principal,

still in a state of shock.

"It's true. It's my business to know such matters. Let us examine the battery."

They went to the Principal's office and took the gizmo apart. They could see that it had been destroyed but could not understand how it had happened.

"We have a mystery on our hands," said the mechanic. "This is not the doing of a mouse— or, if it is, then he is a mouse from outer space."

"Mice don't come from outer space," replied the Principal.

"I believe this one does."

"Perhaps it is radiation, coming up from the ground."

"Impossible."

It was at this point that the Principal began to shake. Her nerves, which were usually very strong, began to twitch. She began to sing the musical scale, which was something she did only when her nerves were tingling. "Doh, re, mi, fah, soh, lah, ti, doh," she sang, looking out the window at the children crowding into the yard.

The teachers began to arrive for class. Mr White, the infant teacher, was among them. He was looking quite pale.

"Well?" he asked. "Have you got rid of the mouse?"

The Principal sang the scale again and said, "Well, yes and no. We believe that we have. At this moment he should be running around the attic, his brain and his memory destroyed."

"But what happened to the famous black box?" he asked, catching sight of it on the Principal's table.

"A slight mishap," the Principal said.

"A flash of radiation, I believe," the owner of the gizmo said.

"A flash of radiation?" Mr White repeated in awe.

"Either that or this mouse has strange magical powers," the gizmo owner said. Mr White and the Principal began to titter, but it was a titter of fear.

A child from fourth class, who had been listening at the door of the Principal's office, rushed out into the playground. "There is a mouse from outer space in the school," he said. "He has frightened the teachers. They are shaking and trembling and I heard the Principal singing the musical scale."

"Hurrah!" cried all the children. "Three cheers

for the magical space-mouse."

Back in the Principal's office, there was confusion. Mr White refused to go to his classroom and the Principal sang the scale up and down several times. Then she pulled herself together.

"Let's take hold of ourselves. We must behave normally. I will call in the pupils. Now remember," she said to all the teachers, "we must behave normally."

The alarm sounded and the children filed into the classrooms. The smell of the melted battery still hung on the air.

Gradually, calm settled on the school. Occasionally a teacher darted from room to room to ask if the mouse had been seen.

But nobody saw the mouse.

At lunchtime, Marcus raided the infants' classroom. He was delighted with the amount of chocolate he managed to find. He ate all he could, and returned to the attic, ready for any attack.

"Teachers should never try to outsmart school mice," he said to himself as he settled down to sleep. He had defeated all his enemies so far and he had wrecked the gizmo.

7

Marcus Saves the School

A few nights later, it was cold, wet and windy. Marcus was asleep. The children, who were smart, had figured out that Marcus needed a supply of chocolate to keep up his energy, so they made sure that he got plenty.

On the night of the storm, his energy level was higher than ever before. He was snoring lightly in the attic when he was awakened by a noise. He listened and looked through the floorboards.

"OK Pete. If she refuses to open the door, pick the lock," said a gruff voice.

"Sure, Bert, it's a piece of cake."

It was obvious to Marcus that two thieves had come to raid the school. He had heard of these two before now—Bert the Bully and Peter the

Pickpocket. The door of the school was opened and a torch lit up the corridor. Marcus quickly scampered down from the attic and saw the Principal being pushed along by Bert the Bully. Bert was very tall, very wide, and had a scar on his face. At another time in history, he would have been a pirate.

The Principal looked very white and frightened.

"Lead us to the safe," Bert ordered.

"And what if I refuse?" the Principal said weakly.

"Bert has ways of making people talk," Pete said. "So if I were you, I'd spill the beans."

Bert let out a loud, frightening guffaw which filled the corridor with evil echoes.

"Very well, I will show you where the safe is," the Principal agreed.

They moved along the corridor by torchlight, as far as the Principal's office.

"Now tell us the combination number of the safe," Bert ordered.

The Principal refused.

"It doesn't matter, boss. Leave it to Pete. I take pride in opening combination locks. I brought my instruments."

He took a stethoscope from his bag, placed it

around his ears as a doctor does when he listens to someone's chest, and put on fine white gloves.

"I'll tie this lady up," said Bert. "She's no good to us. And when we get the money we'll clear out the rest of the place. I reckon there is three thousand quids' worth of equipment here."

"A good night's pickings, Bert."

Marcus did not wait to see the Principal being tied up. It was a pleasure he could not afford. He had work to do, the most important work of his life. It was a long shot but he would have to try it.

He rushed up to the attic and from there he made his way on to the roof of the school. He had gathered all his energy. Now he released it and sent huge charges to his ears.

He flashed out the signals. They lit the sky like lighthouse beams.

Sam the sailor, who had sailed the seven salty seas and had lost an eye in China and a leg in Africa, was looking out the window of his little cottage. It was a long time since he had been to sea.

He looked out at the stormy night. Suddenly he saw the beams flashing. He recognised the signals. "A ship in distress, by the leg I lost in Africa."

The dots and dashes filled the sky.

Sam hobbled to his bedroom and returned to the window with his telescope, which he put to his good eye.

"Couldn't be a ship in distress. This be dry land." He followed the beams. "They're coming from the school." Somebody was sending signals across the night sky.

Sam grabbed his old duffel coat and made his way to a neighbour's house. "There's trouble at the new school," he said. "Will somebody telephone the gardaí?"

Marcus felt faint. He left the roof and staggered back down into the school. In the infants' classroom, he found some chocolate and ate it to boost his energy.

He felt his batteries recharging and rushed along the corridor. When he peeped into the Principal's office, he saw her bound and gagged. She was sitting on a large wastepaper basket and the thieves were just finishing their job.

"Reckon we got three thousand quid here, and the equipment will earn us a tidy bit more," said Bert with a smile. "Let's get moving."

Marcus ran out into the dark yard. He had to

think quickly. As soon as Bert and Pete arrived at the front door of the school, he flashed his ears.

"It's a searchlight. I'm blinded," gasped Bert, stumbling backwards.

Pete let fall the television he was carrying. He put his hands over his eyes.

Then there was darkness.

"I'm blinded. We're surrounded," cried Pete.

By now Marcus had moved to another position in the schoolyard and was flashing out strong beams of light towards the two thieves.

"We're surrounded," cried Pete again. "There are too many against us. We might as well give up."

Bert the Bully knelt on the ground and cried out, "Don't shoot. There are only two of us. We're just ordinary robbers."

It was then that the garda car carrying Sam the sailor and his neighbours arrived. They had seen the bright beams flashing out as they drove up the hill towards the school.

Sam hobbled over to the source of light. He saw Marcus. "Well, shiver my timbers. It is a mighty mouse with mighty power. And he knows the Morse code. He has saved the school from

these thieves."

Marcus smiled as only a mouse with magical powers can. He flashed a coded message to Sam.

I-a-m-M-a-r-c-u-s

"And a very brave mouse you are, Marcus," Sam the sailor said.

Bert the Bully and Pete the Pickpocket, still confused by their dazzling experience, were led away.

The Principal, white and shaken, was released.

"How did you know they were in the school?" she asked her rescuers.

"Marcus the Mouse signalled," Sam the sailor said.

"How did he signal?"

"Through the Morse code."

"Then I must apologise to Marcus," the Principal said. But Marcus was nowhere to be seen.

He had retired to the attic, very weak and tired after his eventful night, to have a good sleep.

8

Marcus the Hero

It was a late autumn evening. The board of management was meeting at the school. The members entered with heads hung down, feeling very sheepish—as well they might!

Marcus the school mouse had become a local hero and a legend in his lifetime. The story of the capture of the thieves was big news in big print on the front page of the national newspapers. It was rumoured that the Disney Corporation was going to make a major film about Marcus. From all over the country, bars and boxes of chocolates arrived at the school. They were stacked in the Principal's office.

The meeting of the board of management began.

It was a most unusual meeting.

Marcus, who had been invited, sat on a book in the middle of the table, eating from a box of chocolates. Opposite him sat Sam the sailor. He had been invited along in order to interpret the Morse code for the board of management.

The Principal began. "We owe a huge debt of gratitude to Marcus for saving the school funds and the school equipment."

"I second that," said the dentist.

"I third it," said the postmistress.

"I fourth it," said the mechanic.

"I fifth it," said the sweetshop lady.

"And I have the pleasure of sixthing it," said the garda, who always liked to have the last word.

"Good," said the priest.

Marcus flashed out a reply in Morse code.

T-h-a-n-k-y-o-u

Sam the sailor translated.

The principal continued. "I now propose that Marcus, because of his great powers, should become guard mouse for the school. This is a government post and he is thereby entitled to an unlimited supply of chocolate."

"I second that," said the dentist.

"I third it," said the postmistress.

"I fourth it," said the mechanic.

"I fifth it," said the sweetshop lady.

"And I have the pleasure of sixthing it," said the garda, who always liked to have the last word.

Marcus flashed out a reply in Morse code.

T-h-a-n-k-y-o-u

Sam the sailor translated.

Marcus continued to flash.

I-a-c-c-e-p-t

There was joy in the staffroom.

The meeting was called to a close.

Everybody was happy.

Marcus returned to his secure home in the attic.

Winter followed.

Often at night, as people passed by the school at a distance, they saw Marcus flashing out the Morse code to his friend Sam the sailor.

Marcus did live happily ever afterwards.

He is still alive.

Long live Marcus.